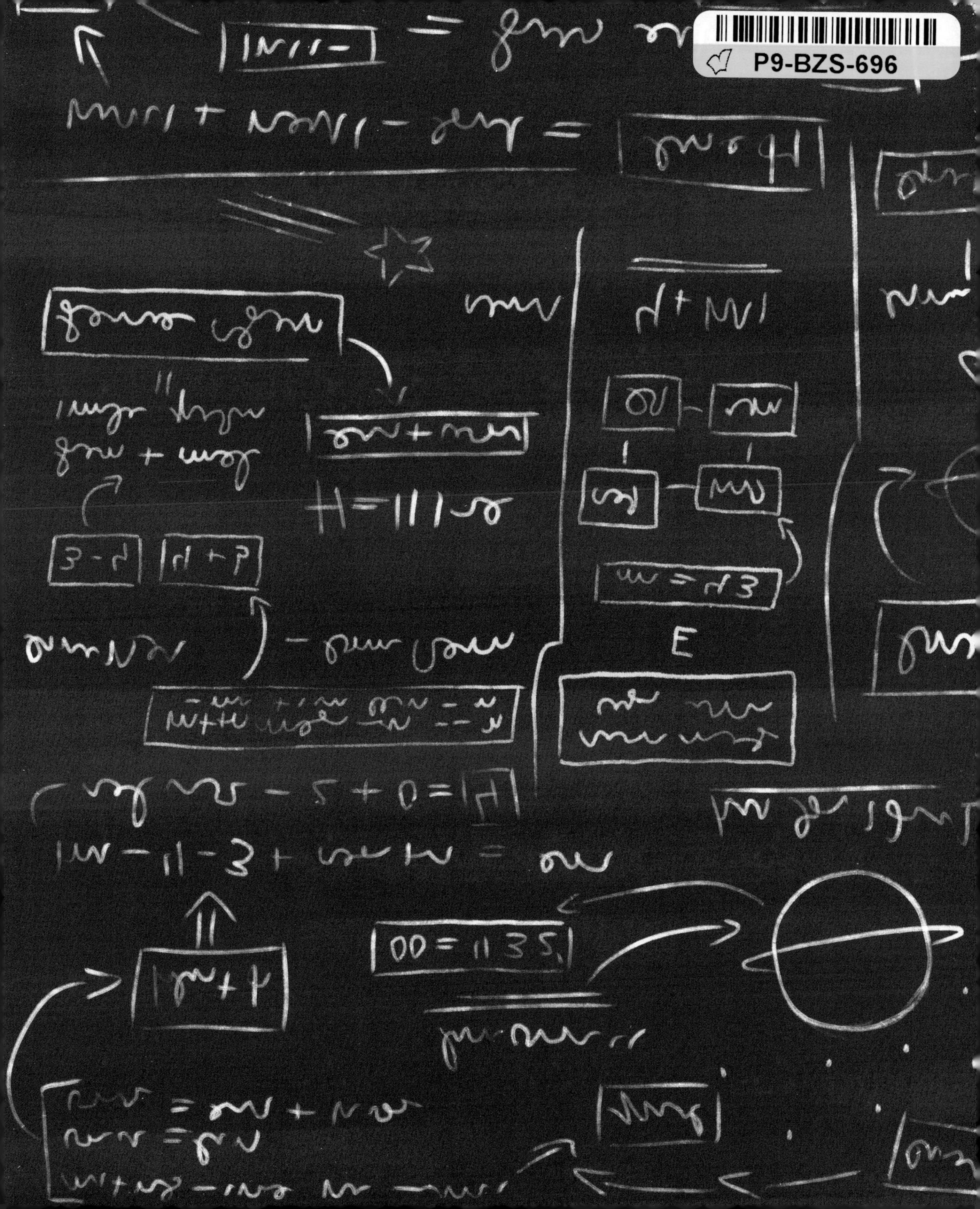

Illustrations by Isabel Muñoz.

Written by Jane Kent.

Designed by Nick Ackland.

WHITE STAR KIDS

White Star Kids® is a registered trademark property of White Star s.r.l.

© 2018 White Star s.r.l.
Piazzale Luigi Cadorna, 6
20123 Milan, Italy
www.whitestar.it

Produced by i am a bookworm.

ISBN 978-88-544-1337-5
2 3 4 5 6   23 22 21 20 19

Printed in Turkey

The life of Albert Einstein

WHITE STAR KIDS

My name is Albert Einstein, and I am a world famous mathematician and physicist.

Throughout my life I asked, and found the answers to, many important questions.

Join me on my journey of scientific discovery, which changed forever the way we think about energy, gravity and the world around us.

$$E = MC^2$$

I was born on 14th March 1879, in Württemberg, Germany. My father, Hermann, was a salesman and engineer and my mother, Pauline, ran the household. Two years after me, my little sister Maja was born. We were a secular Jewish family.

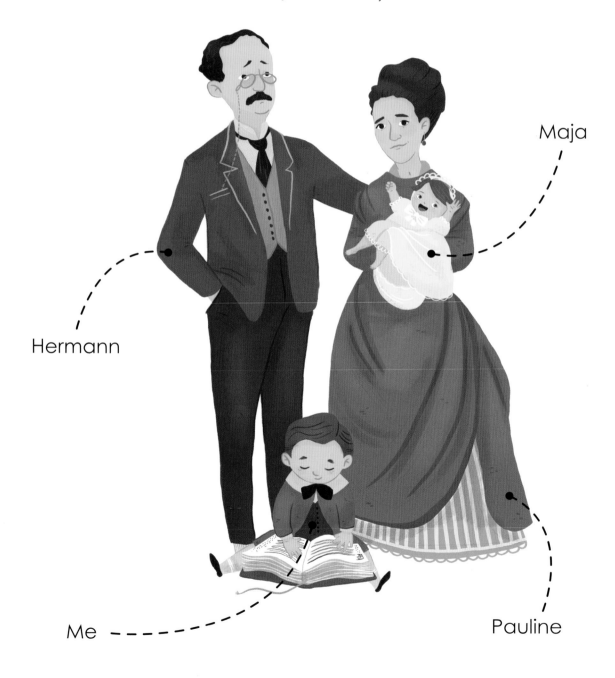

Maja

Hermann

Me

Pauline

Six weeks after my birth, my family moved to Munich and my father founded Einstein & Cie with his brother. It was a company that manufactured electrical equipment.

I went to school at the Luitpold Gymnasium, where I developed a life-long passion for classical music and playing the violin.

In 1896 I applied to the Swiss
Federal Polytechnic School in Zurich.
I passed the entrance exam with flying
colors and began training to become a
teacher in physics and mathematics.
But after getting my diploma, I struggled
to find a teaching job.

Instead I acquired Swiss citizenship and in 1902 accepted a position as a clerk in the Swiss Patent Office. The following year I married Mileva Maric, a brilliant Serbian physics student I had met at school in Zurich, and with whom I already had a daughter. We went on to also have two sons.

During my stay at the Patent Office I had time to explore more deeply some of the ideas I had during my studies at the Polytechnic.

1905 was to be one of the most important years of my career. During that time, I received my Doctor of Philosophy degree and had four papers published in the *Annalen der Physik*, one of the top physics journals at the time. Two of the papers were on the photoelectric effect and the other two were about my special theory of relativity.

To explain the relationship between matter and energy I came up with an equation - E=MC². Energy (E) of a body is equal to the mass (M) of that body times the speed of light squared (C²). This discovery meant that tiny particles of matter could be converted into huge amounts of energy.

Suddenly, I was in demand. In 1909 I was made Extraordinary Professor at the University of Zurich, then a couple of years later I became Professor of Theoretical Physics in Prague. I was appointed Director of the Kaiser Wilhelm Physical Institute and Professor at the University of Berlin in 1914. That same year I became a German citizen again.

I finally completed my general theory of relativity in November 1915. It was the culmination of my life's research! It meant we could more accurately predict planetary orbits around the sun, and explained in greater detail than ever before how gravitational forces worked.

Respected British astronomers Sir Frank Dyson and Sir Arthur Eddington took measurements and made observations during the 1919 solar eclipse. Their findings confirmed my theories, and from then on I was famous in the world of science.

I won the Nobel Prize for physics in 1921. It was for my explanation of the photoelectric effect, where I suggested that light is both a wave and a particle. This phenomenon is known as the wave-particle duality of light, and has influenced the development of microscopes and solar cells.

When particles of light, called photons, shine on a metal surface, they collide with electrons. The photons use some of their energy to knock the electrons loose. The rest of the photon's energy is then transferred to the now free-roaming negative charge, and they are called photoelectrons.

PHOTONLIGHT

PHOTOELECTRONS

METAL

I emigrated to America from Berlin in 1933. I was unhappy with the rise of the Nazi movement, so I gave up my German citizenship for political reasons. I became a United States citizen in 1940. I lived in Princeton Township where I was Professor of Theoretical Physics at Princeton University. The University was an oustanding center for the study of theoretical physics. I worked here until I retired in 1945.

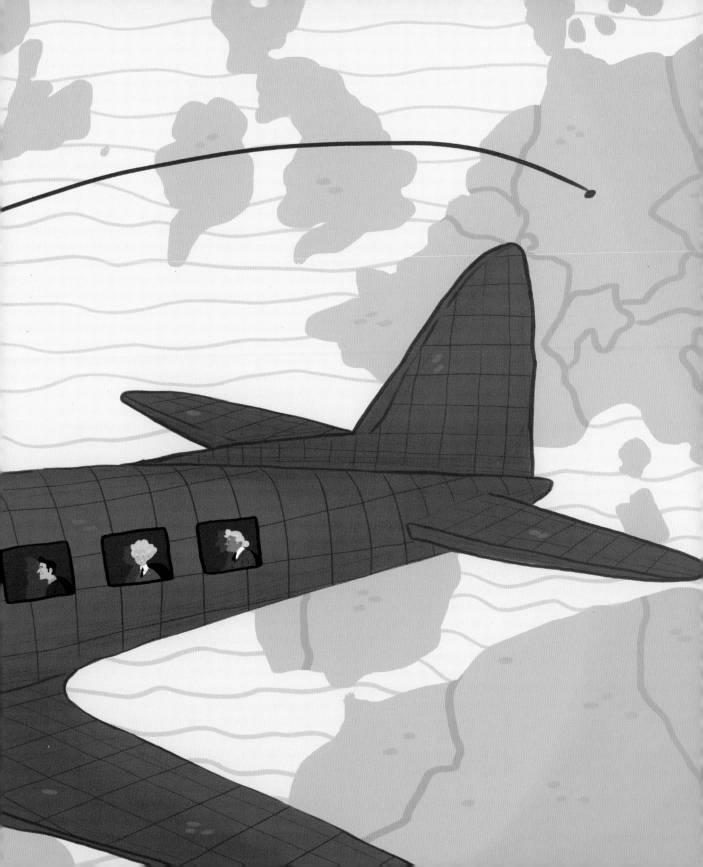

After World War II, I took a leading role in the World Government Movement. I was passionately committed to the cause of global peace, believing that patriotism was often used as an excuse for violence. I considered myself a citizen of the world and so I endorsed the League of Nations, followed by its successor, the United Nations.

Throughout my life I spent a lot of time on my own, pondering and planning. When I did have a spare moment to relax, music really helped to put my busy mind at ease. It also influenced my science work, which I wanted to be harmonious with a sense of beauty.

I had participated in brain studies throughout my life, and wanted my brain to be preserved after my death so that in the future it could be studied by doctors of neuroscience. Thomas Stoltz Harvey did as I wished, and my brain is now located at the Princeton University Medical Center.

In 1999, when Canadian scientists were studying my brain, they found that my inferior parietal lobe is 15 percent wider than it is in most other people.

This part of the brain processes spatial relationships, 3D-visualization and mathematical thought, and researchers believe it explains why I was so intelligent.

My greatest achievements have changed the way scientists of today think and how they approach their work. Every time I made an astonishing discovery, I used it as a stepping-stone for the next one. Have determination, never stop questioning - and finding the answers!

Einstein is born on 14th March in Württemberg, Germany.

He starts teacher training at the Swiss Federal Polytechnic School in Zurich.

His daughter Lieserl is born, and he begins working in the Swiss Patent Office.

PATENT OFFICE

1879

1896

1902

1880

1901

GERMANY

MUNICH

His family moves to Munich.

Einstein officially becomes a Swiss citizen.

His first son, Hans, is born.

He is made Extraordinary Professor at the University of Zurich.

1904

1909

1903

1905

1910

He marries Mileva Maric, the mother of Lieserl.

ANNALEN DER PHYSIK

Einstein receives a Doctor of Philosophy degree and has four papers published, one about his special theory of relativity.

His second son, Eduard, is born.

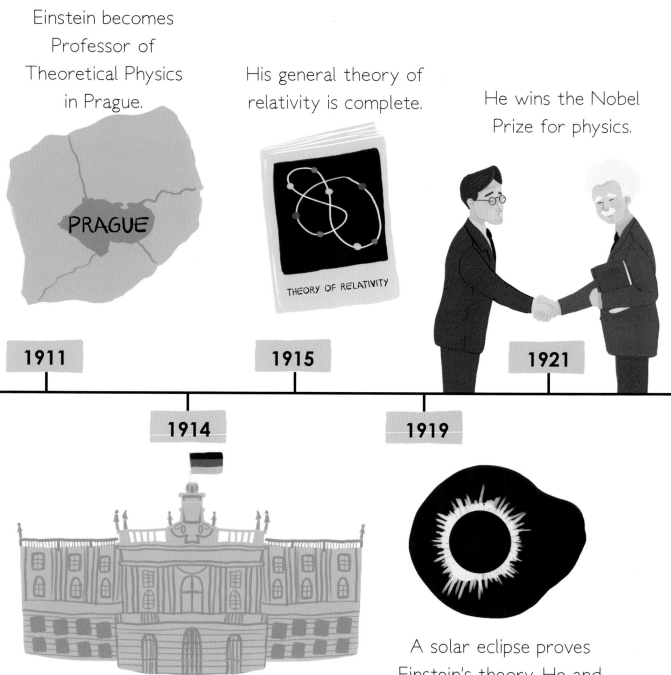

Einstein becomes Professor of Theoretical Physics in Prague.

PRAGUE

His general theory of relativity is complete.

THEORY OF RELATIVITY

He wins the Nobel Prize for physics.

1911

1915

1921

1914

1919

He is appointed Director of the Kaiser Wilhelm Physical Institute and Professor at the University of Berlin, and becomes a German citizen again.

A solar eclipse proves Einstein's theory. He and Mileva divorce and he marries Elsa Loewenthal.

His wife, Elsa, dies.

He retires.

1936

1945

1933

1940

1955

Einstein emigrates
to America.

He becomes a United States
citizen and is Professor of
Theoretical Physics
at Princeton.

Einstein
dies,
aged 76.

QUESTIONS

Q1. In what year was Albert Einstein born?

Q2. What musical instrument did Einstein play?

Q3. Einstein trained to become a teacher
in what subjects?

Q4. What was the name of Einstein's first wife?

Q5. How many papers did Einstein have
published in the *Annalen der Physik*?

THEORY OF RELATIVITY

Q6. What is the equation for Einstein's special theory of relativity?

Q7. Einstein won the Nobel Prize for physics in what year?

Q8. What are particles of light called?

$E=MC^2$

Q9. How old was Einstein when he died?

DR EINSTEIN IS DEAD

Q10. Where is Einstein's brain now located?

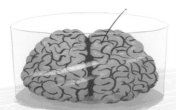

ANSWERS

A1. 1879

A2. The violin.

A3. Physics and mathematics.

A4. Mileva Maric.

A5. Four.

A6. $E=MC^2$.

A7. 1921.

A8. Photons.

A9. 76.

A10. Princeton University Medical Center.